Usborne
RAINY DAY ACTIVITY BOOK

Rebecca Gilpin

Designed and illustrated by
Erica Harrison, Adrien Siroy, Cecilia Johansson,
Laurent Kling and Mattia Cerato

Edited by Fiona Watt

You'll find the answers to the
puzzles on pages 60-64.

BUSY STREET

Colour in the houses and cars along this street.

SPACE

Can you work out which planet this rocket is going to?

It doesn't have a ring around it.
It isn't blue or red.
It has steam coming from it.

Look at the picture below of footprints on the Moon.
Which astronaut made them?

....

Sara   Nico   Felix

Pirates

Join the dots from 1 to 10.
What have you drawn?

Which flag is different? ....

A

B

C

Which way does the pirate ship need to go to reach the island? ....

A SNOWY LAND

Follow all the penguin footprints. Which two penguins climbed out from the hole in the ice?

Emperor penguin

Adélie penguin

Rockhopper penguin

How to draw a seal:

Draw a shape for a seal's head.

Add a nose, and two dots for eyes.

Draw whiskers, and curves for water.

DINOSAURS

Which of these three dinosaurs has the most teeth? ....

Can you spot 7 more dragonflies like this one?

Draw a line to link each dinosaur to its nest of eggs.

Which dinosaur has only one egg?

Who catches the fish? ....

DRESSING UP

Find and colour...

...2 children in monster costumes

...3 balloons

...a girl dressed as a fairy

FOOD

Which two children need to swap bowls so everyone can have what they like to eat?

"I like pasta." "I love tomato soup." "Ice cream is so yummy."

Freya   Leo   Elijah

Read the shopping list below and look at the picture.
What is missing from the picture? Draw a line under the word.

sandwich
bananas
chocolate
oranges
fish
cookies
apples

Who is drinking the banana milkshake?

Tom   Anna   Lottie

Colour this yummy cake.

Draw a flame on the candle that has been blown out.

Draw around each egg's edge. How many eggs are there? ....

BUSY POSTMAN

Ben needs to deliver letters to people on the island, in the order shown below. Draw a line to show which way he needs to go.

Cally | Mrs. Cobb | Ali | Isobel | Dr. Lowe | Dot | Maddy

IN THE RAiNFOREST

Two of these toucans are the same. Can you spot them?

Frogs love the rain. How many can you spot? ....
Draw around each one you find.

These monkeys' faces follow a pattern. Is the monkey on the end sad, surprised or happy? Work it out, then draw its face.

This sloth hasn't moved all day, but some things around it have. Spot and draw around four things that have changed.

ON HOLiDAY

Which way does this family need to go to get to the log cabin?

Who's forgotten to bring a bag? Draw a line from each person to their bag. Then, draw around the person who doesn't have one.

Look at all the people at this campsite. Can you spot what someone is cooking for dinner?

UP IN THE AIR

Draw the faces of more passengers in this plane.

These planes are flying at an air show.
Colour them so that they all match.

How many birds can you spot and colour on these pages? ....

Give the sun a big smile.

Which hot-air balloon lands first? Write the answers to the sums below. The balloon with the highest number lands first.

$4 + 5 =$ .... A

$8 - 1 =$ .... B

$6 + 2 =$ C

MONSTERS

Which monster stole the cake?

It is hairy.
It has horns.
It has more than two eyes. ....

Draw the other half of this monster.

How many spots does this monster have? Colour them as you count them.

....

DRAW A MONSTER

1. Draw a body shape.

2. Add arms and legs.

3. Draw eyes and a mouth.

4. Add horns, scales or spots.

Draw lots more monsters.

ON THE BEACH

Follow the footprints to find out...

1. Who has been paddling in the sea? ....

2. Who has just arrived at the beach? ....

3. Who has eaten an ice cream? ....

Spot and draw around:
2 crabs
5 shells
4 buckets
3 balls

Starting with 1, join the dots to complete the picture.

Draw faces on the starfish.

Which photo has Roberta taken? ....

KNIGHTS AND CASTLES

Can you spot ten differences between this picture...

...and this one? Draw around the differences on this page.

DOGS

These dogs want to meet at the gap in the fence between their houses. Which way does each dog need to go?

Gap

Draw a line to join each puppy to its mother.

CATS

Give these cats ears, whiskers and markings, such as stripes.

Which cat has the most fish in its bowl?

....

Draw a sleeping cat.

1. Draw an oval, then add a smaller one inside it.

2. Draw two paws and a curling tail.

3. Add ears, eyes, a nose, a mouth and whiskers.

33

SPOOKY STUFF

Which of the three monsters below is hiding in the forest? ....

A

B

C

How many bats are there?

....

Complete the face on each pumpkin lantern, then colour them orange.

Can you spot five differences between these spooky houses? Draw around them.

Which ghost is different?

Draw the other half of this vampire. Then, colour him.

IN THE SNOW

Each of these children has a different colour hat. Colour their scarves, gloves and boots to match.

Draw more snowballs flying through the air.

Can you spot three dogs?

How many big snowflakes are there? ....
Draw a face on each one.

Which order should these snowman pictures be in? Number them from 1 to 4.

Follow the footprints to find out where each child has come from.

Bench   Playhouse   Tree

Arthur   Violet   Frankie

FUNNY FACES

Draw the other halves of these faces...

Doodle eyes, noses, mouths, glasses and hair on these faces...

UNDERSEA WORLD

Draw more scales on these fish.

Give this shark more teeth.

Which two starfish are the same?

Make an octopus...

1. Cut a strip from a piece of paper, to make a tab. Draw a line down the middle.

2. Draw three more lines on each side of the first line.

3. Turn the paper over. Draw a face and lots of suckers.

Colour the baby whale to match its mother.

Fill in the turtle's shell.

How many yellow fish are there altogether?

....

4. Turn the paper over. Cut along the lines. Turn the paper over again.

5. Bend the paper around. Then, stick down the tab using sticky tape.

6. Curl each leg by wrapping it tightly around a pencil.

ZOO ANIMALS

Which elephant has filled its trunk with water from the bucket?

Can you spot a sleeping lion?

GIRAFFES

Colour the giraffe to make it match its friend.

How many snakes and lizards are there?

Snakes .... Lizards ....

REPTILES

Can you find a mouse hiding somewhere on these pages?

ROBOTS

Which robot in each of these rows is different?

Put these robots in height order. Write 1 next to the shortest one, and 5 next to the tallest one.

The robots below are helping with the housework. Draw a line to link each robot to the task it will be best at.

cleaning   painting   gardening   cooking

Night Time

Which is the biggest star? Colour it blue. Which is the smallest? Colour it red, then colour the rest of the stars yellow.

How many stars are there altogether?

One of these cats has sneaked out of the house and is prowling along a wall – which one?

It's time for bed, but some lights are still on. To turn them off, use a black pen to fill in all the yellow windows.

Each pair of eyes belongs to one animal. There's an extra animal in the second picture – can you spot it?

Which firefly was on the leaf before it flew away?

AT SEA

Draw more portholes on this cruise ship.

How many of each kind of sea creature will the scuba divers see?

OUT AND ABOUT

Fill in the picture below with pens that match the spots.

Which cyclist is fastest? Write the answers to the sums below. The cyclist with the highest number is fastest.

3 + 4 = ...

5 − 3 = ...

7 + 2 = ...

Which square will complete this scene?

DRAGONS

Complete these dragons with a black pen.

Draw eyes and nostrils.

Doodle scales on the dragons.

Add spikes on their tails...

...and sharp claws on their feet.

IN THE GARDEN

Colour the rest of the fence, following the pattern of colours.

Has every caterpillar below eaten one hole in the leaf?

To help the fly escape the frog, draw a line as quickly as you can, without touching the lines.

How many worms can you see?

....

Which way does the snail need to go to meet its friend?

CARS AND TRUCKS

How many green and yellow cars are there in this picture?

Green cars ....

Yellow cars ....

Draw over the dotted lines to complete the car, then colour it in.

These truck drivers are ready to go to work, but will each of them get a truck to drive? ....

Which truck is the odd one out?

This truck needs to make lots of deliveries. Draw a line taking it to each place, from 1 to 6.

ANSWERS

2-3 SUN AND RAIN

worm

The sun has 8 rays.

Trees 1 and 4 are the same.

6-7 SPACE

The rocket is going to this planet.

Nico made the footprints.

8-9 PIRATES

The bones on flag A are different.

The ship needs to go along route D.

○ twins

○ 3 pirates are asleep.

○ rat

10-11 A SNOWY LAND

The Adélie penguin and the chinstrap penguin climbed out from the hole.

12-13 DINOSAURS

Dinosaur A has the most teeth.

This dinosaur has only one egg.

C catches the fish.

14-15 DRESSING UP

- ⭕ monsters
- ⭕ balloons
- ⭕ fairy
- ⭕ tiger
- ⭕ astronaut
- ⭕ pirate
- ⭕ princess

16-17 FOOD

Leo and Elijah need to swap bowls.

The oranges are missing.

Lottie is drinking the banana milkshake.

There are 6 eggs.

18-19 BUSY POSTMAN

20-21 IN THE RAINFOREST

Toucans 2 and 4 are the same.

There are 8 frogs.

The monkey is happy.

22-23 ON HOLIDAY

The person in the green top is cooking a fish.

24-25 UP IN THE AIR

There are 9 birds.

Balloon A lands first: $4 + 5 = 9$
B: $8 - 1 = 7$, C: $6 + 2 = 8$

26-27 Monsters

Monster E stole the cake.
The monster has 9 spots.

28-29 On the Beach

1 – Emma, 2 – Flo, 3 – Ivan

- ⭕ crabs
- ⭕ shells
- ⭕ buckets
- ⭕ balls

Roberta has taken photo C.

30-31 Knights and Castles

32-33 Dogs / Cats

Misty has the most fish.

34-35 Spooky Stuff

Monster C is hiding in the forest.

There are 5 bats.

This ghost is different – it's smiling.

36-37 IN THE SNOW

There are 5 big snowflakes.

Arthur – tree
Violet – playhouse
Frankie – bench

40-41 UNDERSEA WORLD

🔴 These 2 starfish are the same.
🔵 There are 5 yellow fish.

42-43 ZOO ANIMALS

This elephant filled its trunk from the bucket.

mouse

sleeping lion

There are 4 snakes and 5 lizards.

44-45 ROBOTS

You should number the robots from left to right: 4, 2, 3, 1, 5.

gardening   cooking   painting   cleaning

46-47 NIGHT-TIME

🔴 biggest
🟡 smallest

There are 10 stars.

Cat A is prowling along the wall.

Firefly C was on the leaf.

63

48-49 AT SEA

50-51 OUT AND ABOUT

Cyclist A is the fastest: $7 + 2 = 9$
Cyclist B: $5 - 3 = 2$, Cyclist C: $3 + 4 = 7$
Square C completes the scene.

54-55 IN THE GARDEN

No. There are 4 caterpillars and only 3 holes.

There are 6 worms.

56-57 IT'S RAINING!

○ umbrellas   ○ running boy
○ dogs   ○ green coats
○ bird in puddle ○ man with beard
○ inside-out umbrella ○ girl in red boots

58-59 CARS AND TRUCKS

There are 8 green cars and 7 yellow cars.

No. There are 6 drivers and only 5 trucks.

This truck has more wheels.

This edition first published in 2025. Copyright © 2025, 2015 Usborne Publishing Limited. The name Usborne and the Balloon logo are registered trade marks of Usborne Publishing Limited. All rights reserved. No part of this publication may be reproduced or used in any manner for the purpose of training artificial intelligence technologies or systems (including for text or data mining), stored in retrieval systems or transmitted in any form or by any means without prior permission of the publisher. UKE

WINDPUMPING HANDBOOK

Sarah Lancashire, Jeff Kenna and Peter Fraenkel